MW00880312

# Praise for

## *The Path of Truth*

Andrea has done it again with *The Path of Truth*. She has an uncanny ability to communicate where many of us struggle and how that affects how we live. I was a big fan of the Frank Peretti series back in the eighties about demonic activity in human lives. I appreciate Andrea not spending time here trying to describe how they look, but focusing instead on how they work in our minds and imaginations. You know as Paul said, "I would not have you be ignorant of his devices." She highlights the importance of being all-in and choosing to say "Yes" to God's way. I also enjoyed how she described His grace showing up in a myriad of ways. Well done, Andrea!! You've given me something to really think about when I'm struggling with choosing the right path.

- *Reggie Beasley, Executive Pastor The Crossing Church, Former Executive Project Manager ExxonMobil*

*The Path of Truth* is a gem of a book that packs a powerful punch. Andrea Joy has gotten to the heart of what prevents so many from reaching their true and highest destiny in Christ – the lies we believe. This book unpacks the way those lies take the place of God's voice of truth in every aspect of our lives, while offering real solutions for walking in the freedom that is ours in Christ. It may be tempting to breeze through this little book, but I recommend the reader move slowly through each chapter with a prayerful and listening heart to allow God to speak to you. That is where real transformation will take place.

- *Mary Grace, Digital Marketing Consultant, Public Speaker, Founder of Mary Grace Media - #gracenotes Music & Art – RealTalk with Mary Grace, www.marygracemedia.com*

This will be a wonderful read to share with those who are feeling stuck and are struggling to see the path before them. The message of how our thoughts and internal language actually impact the future is shown is such a gentle way that others will likely be able to receive and apply the necessary elements into their own lives. That being said, *The Path of Truth* spoke into areas of my own life as well. Reading my own battle through the lens of another story was surprisingly helpful...distant, yet close, if that makes sense! This is the sort of tool that will come out of the toolbox again and again, and because of its fluidity and length, it can easily do so. I believe *The Path of Truth* will speak into the lives of the young and the seasoned alike.

*The Path of Truth* is a book of artfully conceived stories illustrating the toxic lies that undermine our souls as well as the truths that will determine our victory. To read this book is to find yourself in its pages and to discover the path of freedom!

*The Path of Truth* will lead you from that dark and confusing way of living which has kept you unfulfilled, overburdened, and running in circles. If you can see and take the steps through this pivotal entrance, you will be led to the destiny God always intended for your life. Even when you have started to walk in truth, there's temptation to go astray, whether it be from old wounds or the lies they speak. Andrea's book will help us all to identify these debilitating patterns and give us the tools to overcome and turn them into victories!

I love this book filled with short, life-changing scenarios. Each one offers the possibility of change which then plants seeds of hope! Before we can walk in authority, we must first believe that we can actually alter the course of our lives. I believe Andrea has given people the key to opening that door, by infusing hope that they can take the first step. *The Path of Truth* is a much needed message for today, anointed to release people from dysfunctional mindsets and into endless possibilities.

# THE PATH OF
# TRUTH

*Stories of The Lies We Believe &*
*The Power to Break Them*

**ANDREA JOY MOEDE**

Unless otherwise indicated, Scripture quotations taken from the Amplified® Bible Classic (AMP), Copyright © 1954, 1958, 1962, 1964, 1965, 1987 by The Lockman Foundation. Used by permission.

ISBN-13: 9781656934536
First Edition.

Published by The Fullness Thereof
P.O. Box 334
Bulverde, Texas 78163

Cover design by German_Creative.
Formatting by Mwaqash.

# Acknowledgements

*Grateful hugs to my little family for being willing to help carry the load of this book, throughout the planning, writing, & publishing process. Your unselfishness allows me to put my hand to God-projects like this!*

*Big thanks to my hubs who has helped me walk the path of truth over our sixteen years of marriage, always calling me back into alignment when I've started listening to lies.*

*And finally, an enthusiastic high-five to anyone and everyone who has had a conversation with me where my final question was, "Who is telling you that? That's a lie!" Our processing through your real-life situations was a huge motivator for me to get this book written and published for others to glean from.*

# Table of Contents

# How to Read this Book

Part I consists of seven fictional short stories, interwoven with the non-fiction background of this concept. If you're committed and serious about eliminating devastating lies and getting the power of truth revved up, this is a must read.

If you've picked up this book while in chaos or crisis, flip to the topical listing found in Appendix I. This section will get you started dismantling some of the most common lies that take people out. There are eternal realities incorporated here, which will give you a basis for aligning your soul with truth. These will set you free.

Finally, Appendix II includes some fun graphic illustrations of everyday practices for living on the path of truth. These seven habits, practiced consistently, will maintain your focus and keep any new lies at bay as well.

*   *   *

Originally, I had wanted to write this book as a "choose your own adventure" of sorts. Did anyone else here read that series growing up? I loved chasing down each option and reading the different results based on what I had chosen.

Despite that desire, as I began this work, I couldn't bring myself to write the results had my protagonists in each short story chosen the path of lies and darkness. I much rather preferred to keep them in the realm of truth and light.

So please, as a favor to me, do the same in your own life. I don't want to have to write those inevitably sad, depressing tales of lives lived bound up with lies. Live and breathe instead on the path and in the light of eternal truth. This is what will unlock all possibilities for you and your family's future!

# Introduction:
# Our Hidden Ability

"Charrrgggeee!" the little boy cries as he races across the playground. His face is fierce with determination as his imaginary battle (and his role as hero) comes to life in front of him. The child in him fully believes he is a powerful person, capable of living out every single one of his dreams. His hopes haven't been dashed, cynicism hasn't set in, and the lies of this age haven't been planted in his heart...yet. For you see, he is living on the path of truth.

Now, let's take a brief time-out to consider instead the posture of most adults. We might shake our heads, chuckle a little, and then dismiss this scene as juvenile. Most of us have "matured" right out of our ability to think and dream big. That's what we think anyway. When in reality, we've bought into one too many lies that have convinced us we are powerless victims in this game of life. Unfortunately, the resulting scope of our influence most likely reflects that.

While intuitively we all know truth when we see it, we also have a very real tendency to slide back into believing lies when life gets tough. Aren't those negative thoughts and memories always the first ones nipping at our heels when we inevitably go through difficulty?

So, can we get it back? This hidden ability we once had that might even now be evading us. It is the possibility to believe we are more powerful than we can ever imagine, that our simple agreement with truth (or with lies) will determine the very course of our life. This holds true for every single one of us. The evidence is all around, as we will see.

Take the terminal cancer patient who believes he will live...and so he does. Or the bankrupt businesswoman who knows the next venture will work...and so it does. And on a smaller, more recent, and more personal level - the nervous middle-school runner who is told by his coach he should medal in the meet that weekend...and so he does.

Unfortunately, there is a flip side: the young woman who has always said she will die young...and so she does. Or the aging man who acknowledges that marriage never works out for him...and so he finalizes his fifth divorce.

Whether you believe it right now or not, the weight of your agreement, towards truth or towards lies, will be the single most decisive factor in any situation in life. We all have tremendous personal authority, and it's time we begin living like we believe it!

# Chapter 1:
# Scarcity or Excess

Walking in to work on a chilly fall Monday, Paul's mind began to race about the looming presentations and deadlines for the week. He'd already had so many rough patches this year, and it was looking like this one wouldn't be any different. His phone began blinking with more incoming messages before he'd even hit the door.

He continued inside, determined to make it to his cubicle before anyone could catch him. Turning the corner, his boss fell in step beside him. *Well, there goes that plan,* he mused. Paul had worked for Cynthia for the last three years; and while she was certainly likable, she also had a reputation for being the most demanding Vice President in the company.

"How was your weekend, Paul?" Cynthia opened kindly. As he debated whether or not to answer honestly or give a polite non-answer, she plowed straight into her requests. "I know you've got that market analysis due today, but I have some meetings coming up with the CEO. Could you take a look at a few things for me this morning?"

Paul's mind began to flicker, as the pressure of this new demand compounded what was already in process. Belying the internal fire he was feeling, he struggled to answer her calmly. "Sure, Cynthia, you know you can count on me." They parted ways, and Paul continued on to his chair, feeling the weight of more work descending on his hunched shoulders.

That's when it arrived, a sneaky dark wisp, as unnoticeable as could be. *You'll never have enough time to get all of this done, Paul. You're doomed to always live this way, with never enough of anything to survive*, the cold voice whispered in his ear. He'd heard these thoughts for as long as he could remember, so naturally he believed them to be his own.

And it wasn't his fault really; this was the way things had always been for him. He could remember times growing up in the foster home with not quite enough food to go around. There were other situations when he had to make desperate attempts to put together matching clothes that didn't have holes in them. Then came college and living on a pitiful, shoestring budget. Paul had never felt as if he had enough, and it wasn't far from the truth. Scarcity was truly the theme of his life.

As a result, he had been determined to change that fact and had worked incredibly hard to get here. So where was here exactly? Paul had successfully finished graduate school and landed an impressive job with a Fortune 500 company. So while money was no longer an issue, now it was time that he didn't have enough of. Would he ever truly be free from this place of lack?

As his computer lit up, Paul began to pull folders from his briefcase. He continued to let the icy words swirl in his consciousness, never outright saying them but not pushing them away either. Then it happened; he opened his email and scanned a note from HR saying that he'd missed writing his performance reviews. This was going to be yet another costly derailment for an insanely busy week.

That's when Paul snapped, and the shadowy mist grew larger and darker. He fumed under his breath, repeating the very words that had been suggested earlier. "I'm doomed to live this way! I will never have enough of anything to survive!" These spoken words only heightened his aggravation. Now more pessimistic words came flying towards him from the dark cloud, wanting to be released from his mouth.

That's when he saw it, over in the corner by the faux plants, a flash of light. As upset as Paul was, he couldn't help but be captured by this spotless brilliance. His eyes adjusted to the brightness and focused in on the orb. He saw that it began to twist and turn until somehow it broadened. Then it opened up into a mysterious, golden path.

It seemed as if he had seen this pathway before, but it had never been so clearly visible. Unbeknownst to him, the gloomy cloud began shrinking and a low hissing could be heard emanating from the center. *You'll always live in scarcity, Paul. Don't forget that*, it offered menacingly. However, Paul was now completely enraptured. His simmering anger from earlier had begun to dissipate. He quickly stood from his seated position and began taking steps toward the immaculate light in the corner.

As he did, his feet froze in place, and he found he could not move ahead. Paul looked down in wonder and noticed that the next step forward was on to a stone marked with a golden footprint. It had the word "sufficiency" on it. He wondered where it had come from, since that was absolutely the last word he would have used to describe his life. As he slowly read the word anyway, the restraints on his legs loosened and he was able to move forward toward the tunnel of golden light.

Like the next domino to fall, a new stone with a radiant footprint appeared. This one was engraved with the word "enough." He read that word as well and continued into the warmth of the glistening light. The cold words of the dark mist were now firmly in his rear view, as he stepped forward onto additional golden stones of "abundance," "plenty," "surplus," and "excess." With each word that crossed his lips, he felt increasingly free and even more emboldened.

Paul could see that the path ahead kept growing brighter and noticeably wider as it went. He desperately wanted to continue onward. He somehow knew that the path would never end as he spoke the words of the golden stones and confirmed what they had to say, rather than those of the cold darkness to which he was so accustomed.

Reality seemed to be running parallel though, and his workday was calling out to him as well. From sheer duty, Paul glanced backward and then swiftly took a step to the right off of the shimmering path. He landed instantly back in his cubicle and was dropped into his black desk chair. Glancing around, it seemed no one else in the office had even noticed his jaunt into that other, golden dimension.

Paul shook his head and ran his fingers through his greying hair, not sure where to begin after the last few unbelievable minutes. There was a refreshing air around him though, and he immediately began prioritizing tasks for the day ahead. He could see a clear path to the completion of all the items on his list, which had not been there before. He smiled to himself, almost in a state of disbelief as to how this day had changed so rapidly. As he began to mentally charge ahead, ticking off tasks, he noticed golden flecks dusting the top of his computer screen.

***

Paul found himself in a tight spot, as we all do sometimes. He had a difficult choice to make. Would he fall back on his old patterns of thinking that were incredibly comfortable and familiar? Or would he take a courageous step towards a different future, which would require something new of him? This future, though unfamiliar, beckoned him onward, up and out of the strain of darkness.

Paul's simple agreement would be the weight on the scale, determining which way the day (for that matter, the week or the year) would go. He could agree with the self-destructive lie of scarcity that had bound him or with an optimistic eternal truth of excess. It was this pivotal moment, which he had to face alone, that would lay out his path yet to come.

## Do I Have Your Yes?

This leads to an interesting discussion surrounding a base-level question I've often entertained. Now you may believe in God, and you may not; but He is as real as the breath you are inhaling in this very moment. This book cannot be written without including Him, because He has changed my life in absolutely brilliant ways.

One part of the running dialogue I've shared with God over the years has been centered on this thought: "Do I have your yes?" So technically that's a question, and God has posed it to me over and over and over again. The first time it came as a bit of a shock, and I wasn't exactly sure what He meant.

Yes to what, exactly? He began to paint me a picture in broad strokes as the days, weeks, and months passed. He wanted to know if I was all in, if I would agree with His plan even if I didn't understand, if I would pick myself up and keep going on the hard days, if my bottom line and ultimate answer would always be "yes." To remind myself, I even bought a copper bracelet cuff with just that word engraved on it.

In the beginning, I thought this question and process were entirely about surrendering and releasing my own plans to follow His. However, now I'm seeing it goes far beyond that initial step. Of course, God wanted to gauge my level of commitment and build my character. But oh friends, following that simple test was when life really started to get good. I began to understand that all God needed for me to be successful in every area of life was my yes. I just had to give Him my agreement with His light, with His truth, with His enormous ways.

You see, God truly has everything else we need, but this is the one thing He does not and absolutely will not control: our choice. So He patiently waits, as our destinies hang in the balance. Will we give our yes to His truth, or will we hand it over to lies? The immense power contained in little old you and I can be unlocked with our affirmative answer to this simple question.

Just like Paul, we will all have many opportunities to give our yes to condemnation, to negativity, to toxicity – all dark paths to be sure. However, we can also make the better choice of throwing the weight of our yes behind light-filled, possibility-infused, God-truths instead.

# Chapter 2:
# Wither or Flourish

Seven-year-old Marissa was so excited for the upcoming Christmas play. She had been practicing her songs non-stop at home. Even her parents had every line memorized at this point. Finally, it was here! Opening night had arrived. As they jumped in to the car to leave, the paralyzing emotion of fear overwhelmed her and she began to wither. This feeling she knew all too well began to slowly fill her chest, depriving her of oxygen.

Noticing her labored breathing, her dad quickly stopped the car and came around to her side door. "Sweetie, what's wrong? What's bothering you this time?" Regrettably, this situation had played out before, and they were all growing a tad weary of it. "I'm so scared, Dad," Marissa began. "I saw a news story about a horrible car accident in a winter storm, and I...I just can't stop thinking about it. What if that's going to happen to us?"

Her mom began to speak soothingly as her dad held her close, and a warm glow began to fill the car. After a few minutes, Marissa felt the color returning to her cheeks and knew the worst was over. "Thanks Mom and Dad; I'm not sure where that came from. I'm so sorry for being a bother. I think I'm ready to go to the play now." As the car drove on, a small dark shadow huddled in the backseat, somewhat diminished but not ready to give up the fight completely.

As Marissa grew older, her battle with the terrifying thoughts continued. Some days her parents were around to help, and she sailed through those struggles just fine. There were other days and nights though where she had to fight the murky clouds alone. The frigid words always seemed to be nearby with foreboding suggestions: *You're never going to make it. Something terrible will happen to you, and you're going to die young.*

She assumed her friends didn't have such thoughts, that they shared anyway. And while her parents were aware of some of the details, she kept much of it to herself. Whenever the darkness was closing in, Marissa noticed she would have a moment of clarity. This was when she could make a choice to shut the panic down before it had gone too far. Occasionally, she would notice a butterfly flitting around her when she was wrestling through the fear.

By the age of twenty-one, Marissa had become quite accomplished. She had continued with her singing and acting and absolutely loved being on any stage. The memories of her night-terrors and panic attacks had all but faded to the edges of her memory. There simply wasn't time to be scared of dying when you're finishing up college and trying to make it in the entertainment industry.

Marissa and her friends were pushing their bodies to the limit, as they stayed up late studying and trained hard for auditions. She began to notice some tingling sensations and numbness in her body, particularly after strenuous dance classes; but she pushed it to the back of her mind. *It's probably just exhaustion and strain. I'll be fine after I get through these last few months,* she thought to herself.

Then one day came the collapse. Hurrying out of her apartment, her legs gave way and she ended up in a crumpled mess on the sidewalk. Some of her fellow students called an ambulance, and she was whisked away almost before she knew what was happening. The next few hours were a whirlwind of tests and a stream of lab coats consulting her chart. Marissa overheard whispered conversations and did her best not to worry, but soon the icy atmosphere had gripped her heart yet again.

*This is it; you knew this day was coming. You'll never walk again. You'll never dance again. Your life will be snuffed out.* The cold voices sent shivers down her spine, as she tried to push back against the darkness that was encroaching. Her parents were out of the country, so this war she would have to wage on her own. Suddenly, she felt a flutter on her cheek, so subtle she could have missed it.

Marissa's big, brown eyes followed the small, floating creature as it danced effortlessly throughout the room. As she watched, the butterfly began to grow, and she saw it was made of translucent gold. It began to climb higher, and the ceiling in her room gave way to a vast blue sky. She wanted to follow the butterfly's path, but the accusing voices continued to scream that her body was broken and that she would be at death's door soon.

The freedom of graceful movement was too much for Marissa's heart, and she made a jumping leap off the bed and managed to catch a tendril of gold trailing from the butterfly. On the tendril was a flowing line of musical notes, which sang of a healthy body, sitting up and strong in the hospital bed. In order to stay attached to the butterfly, Marissa knew she had to sing along with this truth, instead of the idea of a withering body she had subconsciously believed for so long.

Marissa closed her eyes and held on with all her might, choosing to sing that she could be strong again. Another golden tendril, thicker and more intricate, was floating just above her head. This one had a song composed about her walking out of the hospital, more beautiful and fit than ever. She made a lunge for this strand and grabbed it just before it whipped away. She sang along to the new melody. Then further upward they flew, the surroundings growing richer and more beautifully scented as they went.

The grandest tendril on the butterfly dripped with golden oil, as the music notes rang out with the word "flourish" repeatedly into the air. Marissa reached for this strand, raised her voice in song, and let this truth bellow from deep within: flourish, flourish, flourish. The gorgeous sky continued as far as her eyes could see, but she also noticed that her final song had produced a rain of golden dew drops that was blanketing her previous location below.

Marissa's butterfly caught her gaze and began the slow descent from the heavenlies. In short order, she was back in her room, almost as if she'd never been absent. The medical teams were continuing their work, bustling around the bed. She began to notice, however, that discussions of auto-immune diseases, neurological disorders, and other diagnoses began to be replaced with surprised, pleased comments. They all were beginning to note her progress and turnaround.

Simple recovery was now the furthest thing from Marissa's mind, and she continued to mouth the incredible song about her body flourishing. She even pictured herself performing on into the future with great grace and poise. As the evening sun sent its last rays through the hospital window, Marissa seemed to be the only one who could see the tiny butterfly of light circling the room, spreading drops of golden oil in response to every note.

*** 

Marissa had long struggled with a toxic lie about her health and longevity, as many people do I'm sure. Even when buried for years, it would occasionally rear its ugly head to trap her once again. This train of thought had seemed to be her burden to bear, until it reached a breaking point. In that pivotal moment, Marissa saw her opportunity to be free and followed the path upward towards truth.

As difficult as it might have been, Marissa broke with the norms of the hospital and the knowledgeable people around her to fight to align with truth. She was the only one with the authority that could change the trajectory of her life. Her courageous choice to dismiss the darkness began to direct her new path, chock-full of potential and new possibilities.

**What You Believe Will Be Your Experience**

So now, it's our turn. What beliefs have we stood on that have either strengthened or weakened our existence and our future? Have we occupied a thought position that buys into withering or one that sees flourishing? It's a probing question to consider, but one worthy of investigating when the stakes are this high. Because after all, what you believe will end up being your experience.

I have to credit my sister with this section. One day as she was listening to God, this simple phrase dropped into her soul: "What you believe about Me will be your experience." At the time, I believe she had been walking alongside some people who were suffering in multitudes of ways. In moments like these, it is much too easy to start questioning

God and wondering if you will end up struggling with the same issues.

As she was wrestling this out, God in His goodness whispered that thought to her heart. It seemed so simple, too simple in fact to be of much good. Aren't those the concepts though which often rattle our status quo? It's a back to basics thought, that's for sure. I would also add that it is highly Scriptural.

After she shared with me, God was quick to bring to mind the Bible story of the woman with the issue of blood. She was so sick, beyond reach to most. Yet, her faith compelled her to go reach out for Jesus. Her choice to agree with the idea that He was healer literally pulled power out of Him and transformed her body into wholeness. Amidst the throes of people touching Him, Jesus stopped, knowing that power had gone out of Him. What were the words He had for such a woman, brazen in her behavior for the time? He said to her, "Daughter, your faith has made you well; go in peace."

What she believed about Him truly became her experience. Now this is a highly personal concept. We have no idea what is going on in other people's lives, so it really is best not to touch or evaluate their situations. But as for you...I believe He is challenging all of us on what we truly believe.

Often, this can be quite different than what we profess.    Here I am speaking of our core assumptions: ones often formed in pivotal moments or under pressure, ones that would do us good to assess.

We will all go through times as Marissa did when our core beliefs will be questioned and tested by the lies of darkness.  In these seasons, we must decide which way we will lean.  Will it be in the direction of withering lies or in the direction of flourishing truth?  I pray for all of us that it be towards the latter, that our personal authority will be exerted to keep us on the path of light and truth.

# Chapter 3:
# Abandonment or Kinship

Carson heard the door to his daughter's bedroom slam shut, and he sighed deeply. His small, athletic frame hunched ever smaller as he cringed at the sounds of discord coming from his own home. Growing up, you'd think he had already been through this enough. "Will I ever get a break from all the fighting?" he stammered to himself. *No, you won't. All your relationships will be destroyed, and your family will be no more. Deep down, Carson, you know this: you will always end up abandoned*, came the biting reply.

Mentally shoving the depressing thoughts away, he made his way to the kitchen where he began to wash what remained of last night's dishes in the sink. Keeping his marriage together had been so much work over the years, and now tensions with his kids were beginning to rise. *Man, I don't want to be a statistic*, he thought. *Why is my home-life so hard to control*? Carson was incredibly confident everywhere else, but this dark battleground seemed insurmountable.

As his wife walked in with her eyebrows raised, Carson greeted her with a forced, "Fine morning, huh babe?" She grimaced and began her coffee and breakfast routine. He knew family-unit connections were vitally important, and he was determined to change the course for this tribe, for this family. As his mind headed down this discourse to combat the lies, an icy vapor appeared to his left. *What in the world do you think makes you so different? Don't you remember this?*

In an instant, he was back in his childhood home. He could see the red bricks and that awful carpet. Carson heard the reminiscent shouting and yelling, saw the items being thrown across the house, and anticipated the car starting as one of his parents drove away in anger. Of course, he remembered every detail. They don't say kids are impressionable for nothing. As he gazed at this scene in his mind, he struggled to pull away from it, insisting to himself that things could change for the better.

The frigid hands next grabbed another memory and held it close to Carson's mind. *Oh and this one, doesn't this remind you how you'll never be connected to a family again?* Now he was in his college dorm, answering a phone call from his mom. She had called to let him know that she was leaving his dad. This was no surprise, but the stunning swiftness of the next blows took his breath away. "You probably won't mind because you're away, but I'm moving and really not sure when I'll be back. Oh, and your deadbeat dad said he's finished sending you money for rent."

Yanking himself back to reality, Carson scrubbed the frying pan vigorously. "No!" he exclaimed passionately. "That will not be my story," he said as a hushed screech protested his newfound words. At the same time, heavy footsteps clomped down the stairs. "I'm headed out, mom and dad," his daughter threw the words over her shoulder as she walked hurriedly toward the back door. Carson had already reacted terribly to his daughter once that morning, and he wouldn't make the same mistake again.

"Wait, Abby, can I please talk to you?" The chilling presence nearby was determined to double down on its attack, sensing Carson's increased resolve. His daughter barely slowed her pace, clearly choosing not to engage. *See, they give you absolutely no respect! You might as well be alone*, the voice seethed. Carson took a deep breath, willing himself not to lose control, to stay in a place of pursuit of relationship. Instinctively, he took off in a dead sprint and followed her out the back door.

That's when he saw it: a tiny golden leaf, silent as a whisper, floating mercifully his direction. The iridescence was remarkable. Carson couldn't help but surmise this wasn't just any leaf. Dismissing it, he continued down the driveway, still trying to stop Abby from avoiding their connection. Then out of the corner of his eye, came another luminous leaf. This one was larger, with some kind of writing glowing on it. As it drifted downward, Carson read the word "possibilities."

Without knowing why, he gently blew the leaf in the direction of the car his daughter was starting. As the engine began to turn over, it halted, then stopped completely. That couldn't be a coincidence, could it? Quickly now, more leaves began swirling around him. One after the other, they breezed by: "opening," "construction," "connection," "restoration." Carson paused in wonder, then exhaled all of his pent-up frustration at the cloud of golden leaves. The leaves began tumbling, round and round, twisting into a whirlwind surrounding the vehicle. With that, the bitter presence lost the last of its strength and slowly began evaporating.

Abby cautiously opened the car door and stepped out. "Are we really doing this again, dad? Are you actually going to listen to me this time?" she said, oblivious to the golden messages. The largest leaf of all, blazing with the word "kinship" came to rest on Carson's shoulder. He lifted it slowly and gave one final breath of agreement toward this truth. As the leaf was swept away toward his daughter, Carson stepped forward and wrapped her tightly in his arms.

Words didn't feel quite right in that space, just the intentionality to stay present, to believe it was possible to create a new environment for their family. As the two pulled away from each other, Carson saw a newly sprouted tree beginning to grow in their front yard. It was awash with golden light and adorned with countless, fresh sprouts of golden buds. He knew this tree of life represented the truth of what was possible on this new path together.

Carson watched with awe as the brilliant tree continued to climb towards the clouds, curving higher and higher as it grew. His curiosity was piqued, as its grandeur and glow continued to expand. What was written on those many golden leaves, now creating a rich canopy above their home? The prospects flashed like a slideshow before his eyes. These were hopeful images of a family woven together in kinship, never to live in abandonment again.

The preciousness of the vision was so unexpected and refreshing, like a cup of cold water in the desert. So much so, it kicked off a flurry of teardrops in Carson's eyes, which began to drop to the ground one by one. His fears of being alone were melting away as the seconds passed. Abby grabbed his hand and brought him out of his momentary, golden daydream. "Alright dad, you don't have to turn on the water works. I'll hear you out; let's go inside."

\*\*\*

Carson has been saddled with a heartbreaking history of family baggage. Unfortunately, back stories like these can be a prime access point for darkness to begin its attack. Our personal pain practically attracts more self-perpetuating lies, which then end up causing more pain and continuing the dysfunction. That is exactly where the lies would have us stay.

However, more than any of our other characters so far, Carson was actively fighting internally to chase after the standard of truth he longed for in his family. He wanted kinship instead of abandonment. While others present may never see this important battle rage, the results will likely end up manifesting eventually in our lives. The path of our existence will begin to reflect what we have been choosing: truth or lies.

## The Smallest of Our Internal Choices Are Pivotal

So which direction do our habitual internal choices lead, following the light or heading back into darkness? Your situation may not be as cut and dry as Carson's story (it rarely is). However, if we take a step back from the details, we can often see a clear pattern of thinking that has been guiding us. Follow these moments like markers on a trail, and it's not too hard to predict where we'll end up. Our lives will literally pivot around the smallest of agreements made with me, myself, and I.

I've had priceless conversations with people who have battled cancer and other terminal diseases. One friend in particular said something a few years ago that stuck with me. She said, "In the middle of a battle like that, no one knows what is happening in those intimate conversations with God." Someone may talk until they are blue in the face about how they are believing for healing, but deep down they've already resigned themselves to passing away. In contrast, you may have someone else who is constantly complaining of their difficulties and pain, but yet they have fiercely determined they will not die.

This paradox can leave those of us left behind with so many lingering questions, because we truly do not get to see the deep internal choices that are happening. Alas, we are not privy to the processing of others, which is morphing and changing moment by moment. This is a compelling reason to never base what you believe on the circumstances of others.

Of course, we must walk through difficulties in life with many people, but their posture and their results (if you will) can never become part of our baseline truth. Each one of us must determine for ourselves what we believe to be true about God and our circumstances. These private places we establish will be the fulcrum around which our lives will turn.

I remember hearing Shawn Bolz describe the testimony of his physical healing from years ago. He had contracted a deadly parasite, and his body was not able to fight it. He had multiple doctors telling him he had only weeks to live. He described something similar to what my friend said above. God pretty simply asked him if he wanted to live. Shawn's response was a quiet "yes" within himself.

He said he didn't have the energy to go around shouting Scripture. He just made a choice that he was going to live, rather than agreeing with sickness and the doctor's reports. Sure enough, following that decision, the healing to his body began. From the outside looking in, you would have missed the shift. It was centered on his internal choice, the weight of his personal authority, to live.

So, when the lies and negativity come toward us in life, as they did Carson, we must pay attention. How are we handling our personal authority? Are we carelessly lending it out to any thought that comes our way (hello infomercials, social media, etc.)? Or are we intentional to manage our internal state? This involves regularly tossing out the lies and persistently coming into agreement with truth instead. The smallest of our internal choices will truly prove to be pivotal.

# Chapter 4:
# Unworthy or Priceless

Ariana stumbled out of the bar, barely able to keep her footing. She couldn't believe all that had just transpired. What began as a fun evening with friends had turned into one of the most humiliating experiences of her life. Almost on cue, here came the voices. *Wow, you really are that lame,* said one icily. Another chimed in, *You're not worth anyone's time – you'll never really belong anywhere.*

She tapped her fingers on her temples as the thoughts invaded. Grabbing her phone, she called for an uber. At least she would soon be out of the embarrassment of the street and in her own place where she could let it all out in peace. What was it about her that was so detestable anyway? She had done everything she could think of for these people, and all they had in return for her was scorn.

Ariana climbed into the backseat of the van, barely acknowledging the driver. It had all started when her friends invited her to a pub crawl downtown. She decided to invite her boyfriend as well. They hadn't hung out very much socially, but she felt like their relationship was getting to that point. They arrived together to the first pub and saw their group already downing their first beers.

"Hey you guys, wait up for us, and we'll join you," Ariana shouted excitedly. As she turned to the bartender, her boyfriend headed to the table. Out of the corner of her eye, she noticed him giving an extended hug to one of the women who was with them. It seemed a little odd, but she brushed it off and continued opening their tab. Carrying their drinks to the table, she noticed one of her friends smirking. "Sure seems odd that you're always the one picking up the check," she said pointedly. The muffled laughter around the table was hard to miss. Ariana's cheeks turned fuchsia, as they always did when her insecurities were revealed.

Her boyfriend put his arm around her stiffly, and she tried to find some comfort in that gesture.

As the drinking continued however, more and more of the jokes seemed to be at her expense. After another half hour, Ariana stood up to take a breather in the restroom. Gazing in the mirror, a small dark cloud appeared. It took its time circling her head, preparing its best taunt yet. *You're simply not good enough. What made you think these people could actually be your friends?*

The words sank in, and she swallowed them hook, line, and sinker. Her only response was to wash her hands, put a little more lipstick on, and hold her head up high. She gave herself a once-over and then vowed to hold her bluff of self-confidence for the rest of the night. Returning to the table, she now saw her boyfriend cuddled up close to the same woman he'd hugged earlier. Ariana began to sputter accusations, but there were no words. She began to feel nauseated, as if someone had punched her in the stomach.

He jumped to his feet and grabbed her elbow, trying to steer her to the corner for some privacy. Ariana was having none of it. "What are you doing? Are you, are you...cheating on me?" His face told her everything she needed to know, as he hung his head in shame with no answer to come. Hot tears began pouring down her cheeks, and she rushed to the table to grab her purse. A few of the girls had sympathetic looks, but most were obviously holding back their glee.

Wincing as she recalled the last few hours, Ariana laid her head back in the uber and fought the next frigid suggestion floating her way, *Stupid, stupid, stupid, why would someone like him ever really care for you?* This thought was now physically causing her pain, like a thousand knives stabbing her all at once. "No more, I just can't take anymore," she whispered in anguish. In that instant, she caught the uber driver's eyes. Instead of judgment and mockery, she saw compassion and kindness. As unexpected as that was after the treatment she'd just endured, what came next really shocked her.

Small golden flames began flickering along the ceiling of the vehicle. Ariana followed the glow with her puffy eyes; it danced in a peaceful rhythm all its own. In one particular flash, she thought she could see the vague outlines of a picture. It began to come into focus and revealed an image of herself, clearly single yet clearly happy. Her face was radiant, and her heart was alive with its own dreams, unconcerned with what others were thinking or doing. Was this even possible? Could she reach that place of confidence? As the glittering flame licked upward and away, she gasped, not wanting that hopeful image to leave her.

Speaking softly, she began to verbalize what her life would look like if she were contentedly single and daring to live again, as depicted in the dazzling flames. As the words were uttered, she felt her shoulders immediately relax and suddenly she could breathe a little easier. Right away, the icy mist that had been following her began collapsing from within.

Whoosh, another larger flare replaced the last. This one had glimmers of gold but also many other rich colors. Ariana peered deeply into the fiery picture as it flickered along the roofline and saw herself approaching a throne embedded with countless jewels. One who appeared to be the King smiled warmly as she ascended the steps and then gestured towards the many gems. "Pick one," he said kindly, gazing at her as if she were the only other person alive.

Ariana knew her favorite instantly. It was a multi-faceted deep blue stone that was situated just on the side of the grand chair. Within a moment's time, the gem emerged from the throne and floated over to the King, who placed it lovingly in an ornate tiara. The King approached her and showed her the inscription: "To Ariana, the priceless jewel, may you always know your true worth."

As she pulled herself out of the gleam of this flame, she wrestled within. *What a beautiful picture, although a touch predictable, and maybe a little grandiose,* she thought. *My imagination's really getting away from me; the possibility of that being my reality is far-fetched indeed.* Her cynical musings caused a twinge of remorse, but then the flame began to burn brighter and brighter. It was as if it wanted her to choose it and the golden picture it held, but the ball was in her court to decide.

It felt like a ping-pong match in her brain, back and forth: unworthy or priceless, unworthy or priceless… unworthy…or priceless… Mustering all the grit she could, Ariana bolted upright in the seat and yelled, "Priceless!" With that, the uber driver let out a victorious laugh, "There you go, girl." Ariana smiled back at him and returned her gaze to the fiery silhouettes. She saw the tiara begin to descend on to her head, then watched the continuing parade of her coming hope and future before her eyes.

*** 

Ariana truly knew rejection. She was intimately acquainted with what it felt like to give everything you have and be left wanting. Like many of us, she had let her heart burn for the wrong things. These people and places took her down a deceptive, lying road that had ended up labeling her worthless. Consequently, she had owned that lie for far too long.

But what if what she was looking for was actually chasing her down all along? What if her esteem and priceless value were wrapped up in her agreement with the truth instead? She would have to exert her will though. That old label wasn't just going to fall off on its own.

## Free Will Is the Most Powerful Thing We Have

It is kind of mind-blowing when we realize how powerful we are. The God of the universe, source of galaxies upon galaxies, saw it fit to give all of humanity our own free will. We can choose where to work, where to live, who to be in relationship with, when to have children, how to manage our time, etc. We can even decide we don't want to believe in the very Being who created us. If I were in charge, I'm not sure I would have put that option on the table; but He did.

He respected our individuality, our space, and ultimately the selection of our eternal destination: with Him or without Him. We need look no further than our enemy for a Biblical example of this.

Lucifer (Helel), the son of the morning, was the pinnacle of created beings as a beautiful angel. However, that simply wasn't high enough for him. Instead of burning for the Almighty One, he began to rest his eyes, focus, and free will on himself and obtaining more glory instead. So, God gave him what he wanted, an eternity outside of His presence. Now we are all dealing with the fallout of that tragic decision and demise.

Since we don't really fathom the level of our authority, we often twiddle away our power by exerting our wills toward unimportant and even worthless things. So the impact and reach our our lives becomes unimpressive, focusing on minor things like controlling situations or other people. Then when the stakes are quite high, as in a major health battle or deep identity question, we don't consider our free will to be much of a weapon.

I believe this discussion with you is part of the wave that will turn the tide though. The atmosphere will begin to be pregnant with the possibility that our God-given free will is the most potent ammunition we have. Further, as we begin to understand this, we will refuse to be distracted by smaller battles vying for our attention. Instead, we will point our collective will at the heart of the matter: bringing the truth of God (and the resulting glory) to earth as it is in heaven. Get ready world; we're about to be unleashed in ways never seen before.

Just like Ariana had to exert her will and make a foundational change in her thinking, we will all be faced with similar decision points. I am sure that when we do and point our free will towards truth, we will know what it feels like to burn for the right things. In turn, this will be the catalytic fireball that sets us free from self-occupied lies of unworthiness. After that, we will be released into our priceless value, only found on the path of truth.

# Chapter 5:
# Useless or Valuable

*Just a few more, and I'll throw them away forever*, thought Bruce. The pills helped him get through the day, but he knew it was only a matter of time before he got caught. He grabbed his water and washed them down as quietly as he could. Then throwing the bottle back into his briefcase, he emerged from the bathroom stall. *You're weak; you can't even stand up to yourself*, the icy voice whispered. *It's a wonder you stumbled into a good profession...otherwise you'd be useless.*

The accusations pestered him like fruit flies that wouldn't abandon a piece of watermelon. He struggled to fight them off, so his mind would be free to get back to his work day. "Hey Bruce, you've got a consult at the window, and then I have several scripts for you to review," his assistant said. Sighing, he put his game face on to do his least favorite part of the job, customer service.

As the afternoon wore on, a pit started to develop in his stomach. Something didn't feel quite right, so he headed back to his office in the corner. He dug around in his bag nonchalantly, silently searching for the comforting shape of the pill bottle. A few seconds passed, then a few more; he couldn't seem to find them. He tugged at the collar on his coat and felt his face begin to grow warm.

*Stupid, stupid, stupid, now you're really in trouble*, said the chilling voice he had come to dread. He was sure his responsibilities were starting to pile up outside, but he absolutely had to find that bottle. Bruce began to retrace his steps and ended up in the hallway to the restrooms. The men's door opened outward, and another employee stood before him. "Were you headed back to get these?" he asked, rattling the pills.

Days later, Bruce woke up groggily in his bed, the memories of the last week rushing back to his consciousness. It hadn't taken management long to assess the situation and fire him immediately. After all, they couldn't have one of their lead pharmacists addicted to pain killers. And while most of his fellow employees liked him, they were unsurprised by the turn of events that had sent him packing.

The thoughts that used to pester were now downright tormenting. Being alone can do that to a person. Like a revolving door, movies of his failures had played on a screen in his mind. He coped the only way he knew how and had ended up passed out, isolated and defeated. Somehow his body had recovered, flushing out the toxic chemicals and allowing him to wake once again. *What, you're still here? Surely a loser like you is ready to quit life, especially now since you've lost your job and are completely useless,* the frigid claims began.

Grabbing as many pillows as he could reach, Bruce buried his head, desperately hoping that would block out the torture as well as the sunlight coming his way. As he rustled under the covers, his hand brushed against something cold and metallic. *Well that's odd*, he thought. *What could be under here?* His fingers felt the shape and knew it to be an old-fashioned key.

He pulled the object out, and the light glistened as it reflected off the golden key. It was well-worn, with many nicks and scratches, but he noticed some deeper grooves on one side. He turned it over and read the word that was engraved, "valuable." Bruce let out a sarcastic laugh. "Well, isn't that just a cruel joke?" he said. Looking at that word was like staring across a chasm for him. He didn't think he could make the leap from the veritable cliff; it was simply too far from what he believed.

Instantaneously, the key began to burn in his hand, and the word's letters lit up brighter than before. Bruce was forced to drop the key as it began to singe his palm. To his utter amazement, the golden key grew and began to hover in midair above a tremendous gorge that had just appeared in his room. As he gazed across the expanse, he noticed smaller keys appearing that formed an arc across the sky to the first key. Each of them had a ring at the bottom that might just be a perfect hand-grip.

His eyes followed the impossible path, and he felt like a first grader again, staring up at the challenge of the playground monkey bars. It didn't seem reasonable to jump off this cliff, but his heart was burning within him. He simply had to have that key back. *No, Bruce, don't get your hopes up. Things will never change for a worthless guy like you*. The bitter voice was nearly shrieking in desperation now. For the first time Bruce realized, it was more scared than he was.

The first key ahead said "useful." Well, at least he could wrap his brain around that one. Forcing himself to look at the keys and away from the potential drop below, Bruce pulled himself upward with his strong right hand. The accusing voice continued to scream, but it began to fade, like a train in the distance. The next key was inscribed "serviceable." He reached for it with his left arm and climbed with ease. Then came the keys saying "helpful," "worthwhile," and finally "beneficial." With each swing forward, the glistening light coming from the original key would brighten, and Bruce felt his hard veneer begin to crack.

After coming so far, that last key didn't seem so challenging, as it loomed in front of him. He rested a bit and allowed his body to sway back and forth, while he gazed down at the golden valley below. It seemed to contain scenes from his life scattered here and there, every one now taking on a different hue as the golden light washed over it. On the top of one small hill was the time his grandfather had said he was nothing if he didn't have a good occupation that contributed to society. Over by a grove of trees was the time in high school when all his friends turned on him, because the project he had completed for them received a failing grade.

The gleaming light was having a strange effect on each situation, adding in new shadows and colors he had not known were there before. There were truths shining like gems that had been covered by a dark mist. The shimmers of light were now pushing the murky clouds away, unveiling the reality of what had really been there all along. The jewels seemed to be reflections of who he was, not what he did. Bruce could see his intrinsic value ostentatiously on display, regardless of his performance in these times past.

Pulling himself away from the grandeur of the view, Bruce knew he had one final swing to make it to the end of this path…valuable…he was valuable. As he grasped the last ring in his hand, he felt a flying sensation. The key had jolted out of place and begun soaring through the air. Bruce flew around and around the gorge, laughing and enjoying the sight while astounded at the transformation that had taken place in his inner world.

Bruce glanced down at his bed, which appeared so small and far away. It was certainly unappealing to return there considering his current state. Just off in the distance though, he could barely see other gorges and their surrounding cliff walls. They looked like they were still shrouded in gloom and the absence of light.

Staring upward at the massive key, he wondered if he could take its golden glow with him to others in the next valley.

***

Bruce felt the emotion of one particular lie that had immobilized his life: he was worthless if he wasn't productive. While I'm sure some women feel this untruth as well, it does seem to be aimed at men more often than not. The devastation of this lie is the inevitable crash that comes when what you 'do' is taken away for one reason or another – job loss, injury, retirement, etc.

The insertion of truth was the key that could unlock his heart to finally grasp his identity as valuable, regardless of the circumstances. The key was there and available for the taking, but he had to take the risk. Bruce had to make the leap from solid footing, from the thought patterns that had grounded him throughout life, upward and into the truth of different possibilities.

## The Cliff Is Where the Momentum Shifts

Have you ever felt yourself arrive at a similar ledge? It's the place where what you've always believed has failed you. You've literally reached the edge and can go no further. Out of desperation, you're finally open to another way, as scary as it may be.

While the initial jump from the cliff does take courage, I also believe that our thought transformation doesn't have to happen in one fell swoop. God is far more gracious than that. He will give us stepping stones, clues in the right direction, to where we begin renewing our minds one small truth at a time. Once we choose to take that first step, God meets us in the cavern of space and time to catch us before we fall.

The clip from the *Indiana Jones* movie of him stepping out onto the invisible bridge comes to mind. For those who missed this epic, the hero is on a quest for the Holy Grail. He reaches a point where there seems to be no path forward, except for a gaping hole in the cave. The clue that led him there said, "The path of God: only the leap from the lion's head will he prove his worth." Indiana stands there struggling with the impossibility of crossing the chasm, before closing his eyes and taking one giant step forward. And wouldn't you know it? There was a bridge there all along; he just couldn't see it.

Take a moment to consider the question: what is the daring and hopeful truth we've been afraid to accept? Is there a step we can take towards it? It may be as simple as standing in front of the mirror and telling ourselves the truth. Whatever this first step is, it will be the catalyst that leads to breakthrough.

One added benefit of launching out on this leap of faith is a new and higher vantage point. There's just something about reexamining our pasts in light of new understanding that is incredibly productive. Taking time to reflect on the arc of our lives with truth as our lens will bring much freedom, healing, and perspective. We only get this view though when we leave the ground.

So friends, when we come to the cliff's edge that is the end of ourselves as Bruce did, yet dare to move forward with courage, the momentum has already shifted in our favor. It is at this very moment when lies begin to lose their hold forever. From that new place, it only becomes a matter of walking it out, truth overtaking our souls a little at a time.

# Chapter 6:
# Dismissed or Unleashed

Isabelle felt the sun on her back before it hid behind the clouds, and she slowly paddled her board away from the rocky shore. It was looking like it might get a little stormy today, as the billows began to gather. This suited her just fine, because it matched what was happening internally. She'd had quite a week, consumed with job hunting and the ever-mounting pressure of being a single parent.

She'd been tempted to hit the club scene, but her previous experiences reminded her to stay on the straight and narrow. *Those mistakes are going to follow you the rest of your life. Why bother cleaning yourself up now?* she heard the frosty finger-pointing begin. Isabelle reached down and splashed some water on her face in an attempt to wash away the voices. As she eyed the horizon for her next wave, she began to replay all of the interviews she'd had recently.

"Wow, you have quite a resume," they began. "But what is this about a drug possession charge on your record?" Isabelle's face reddened, and she started stammering, "Well yes, I was a young college student at a party..." Her explanation sounded absurd, and their faces didn't look like they were buying it anyway. Her self-defense mechanisms kicked in, and she rushed through the rest of the questions to get out of that room as soon as possible. *Dismissed yet again, won't you ever learn? No one is going to give you a second chance*, came another icy arrow aimed straight at her heart.

The following interview hadn't gone much better. The company had immediately honed in on her criminal record, specifically her DUI, instead of any education or experience she had built since then. It was during that embarrassing discussion when Isabelle decided it was time to give up on master's level positions and just search for something with lower requirements. *That's right*, the frigid whispers said. *Your time has passed. You may as well find a job to make ends meet, because you'll never be able to succeed now.*

Paddling furiously, Isabelle lined up her board while an enormous wave approached. She pushed herself to standing, and her muscular legs bent down into a comfortable stance as the water rushed beneath her. There, for a moment, the wind in her hair and salt water in her face provided temporary relief from the emotional anguish of her life. The shadowy haze was determined to land a final blow, so it gathered steam to make an approach once again.

*What about your dating life?* the bitter words flung her way. *None of those men want anything to do with you once they learn about your mistake.* She pictured the beautiful face of her six year-old. That little one couldn't possibly be a mistake. She was more accurately the only thing that could have saved Isabelle's life from self-destruction all those years ago. "Enough," she yelled and waved her arms frantically over her head, trying to shoo away the torment. Amidst the flailing, she lost her balance and splashed violently into the ocean.

Sputtering, she rose above the water quickly, before another wave took her back under. Isabelle fought the undercurrent, kicking to the surface. As she was about to come up for air, an almost imperceptible flash caused her to jerk to the right. *What was that,* she wondered curiously. Her eyes struggled to focus in the tumultuous water. Now she could see that it was a large bubble drifting away from her, but it was unlike any she had ever seen before. It was made of the most beautiful, most translucent gold. Sparkling all around the outside, she saw the letters of her name scrolled out gracefully.

Isabelle made it over to the bubble with a few smooth strokes and just watched for a moment. She finally reached out to give it a light touch, and suddenly it popped. She was astonished to hear sounds emerge, which seemed to have been trapped inside the bubble. She heard a sort of enchanting music, but it was muddled like all sounds underwater. As she listened, a garbled mix of drum beats began pounding, repeating the word "acknowledged" over and over while the glittering fragments of the bubble floated towards her.

Isabelle managed to trap a small piece of the transparent gold between her fingers. As she held it, she felt an urge to sing along with the music. "God, I've been dismissed for a long time. Wouldn't this change be a bizarre turn of events?" she thought to herself. *Impossible!* the condemning voice screeched. The shard from the bubble began to weigh heavier in her hand, forcing her to swim so she wouldn't sink. The other pieces continued to rise in the water, engaging her vision and challenging her thinking. Isabelle looked from those shimmers down to the one she was holding, which had begun to grow darker and was pulling her further under. Instantly, she forced herself to grab hope instead of doubt and mouthed the word "acknowledged."

As she did, the remains of the bubble glowed brighter and brighter and began to multiply before her eyes. Each one was grander than the one that preceded it. Isabelle swam over and began to pierce each bubble with her little finger. As they exploded, she heard a symphony of sounds that rang out with the words "accepted," "freed," and "untethered." The drumbeats of the music were like nourishing food to her hungry soul. She closed her eyes and floated among the shimmering pieces, allowing the sound to become a part of her.

Isabelle's body relaxed as she drifted under the water, and fresh pictures of her mistakes began to transform in her mind. They went from being covered by a filter of gloomy regret to one of hopeful assurance. She then began to see others who had traversed these same places, burdened down with the shame of it all. More than anything, Isabelle wanted her new filter of promise to cover all of these downtrodden ones as well.

Opening her eyes and looking up, she saw one massive bubble remained very near the surface.

Taking one last look around, Isabelle began to swim upward gaining speed with her arms extended. She burst the bubble with her hands, releasing a decisive roar. "Unleashed!" she heard the rhythm express with a tone of finality, as she broke through the surface of the water. The clouds had moved out, and the afternoon sun shone down on Isabelle as she caught her breath in the salty air.

Imperceptible to the world around her, the rhythm kept reverberating in Isabelle's chest. As she hummed along, "Unleashed, unleashed, unleashed," she wondered what the future would hold. While she wasn't certain, she knew it would be vastly different from here on out. Recalling the applications she'd recently completed, her heart began to beat with a newfound confidence and expectancy of what was possible. She also pondered where she could find others like herself who needed this fresh perspective. Isabelle smiled heavenward and began paddling over to retrieve her board.

Back on the shore, Isabelle's cell phone began buzzing and lighting up in her shorts pocket where she'd happily left it behind. It was alive with life now, ablaze with new notifications coming in, with more prospects and potential than she ever could have imagined.

\*\*\*

Isabelle's path had been full of poor choices to be sure.  We've all been there unfortunately, and it's often these times when we are primed and ready for demoralizing lies to attach.  She was already being so hard on herself and having difficulty forgiving the mistakes of her past.  This internal struggle practically painted a target on her back for the lie of dismissal to attack.

If she couldn't let her own missteps go, how could anyone else?  Or at least, that's what the cruel voices said.  However, she only needed to see the flip side of the coin: the truth that these mistakes could be forgiven and were in fact what had made her.  She could be accepted despite all of these things.  And in a happy twist, they would also be the vehicle by which her influence could be unleashed into the world.

**Scary But Trustworthy**

Why is it so much easier to cling to what we know, even if it's damaging us, rather than opening our minds to something new?  I know I've been at that place before like Isabelle, when the lies were literally beginning to pull me under.  I vividly remember though, I still found it incredibly difficult to pull myself out of the tailspin.

Perhaps the most vital missing ingredient here is courage. Humans are nothing if not creatures of habit, and it's far easier to stay where it is safe and predictable. Nevertheless, if we ever want things to change, we're going to have to face the scary reality of heading out into the unknown. I feel like most of us get stopped here at this point. We never take that first step away from our natural thought patterns, so we literally end up in a repeating loop for our entire lives.

Although once we do make that first move, often we find just how trustworthy the truth can be. I want us to really stop and think about this. When was the last time you insisted on rejecting your comfortable lie about a situation and forced yourself to follow truth instead? As squirmy as the situation may have gotten, have you ever been let down when you've traveled this path?

It makes me think of all the stories in the Bible of person after person who took a scary step into truth, into their real identity, and the future that transpired after that. Moses was a stutterer and became a deliverer, Gideon was a chicken and became a mighty man of valor, Rahab was a prostitute and became an ancestor of Jesus, Matthew was a cheat and became a disciple of the gospel, Paul was a murderer and became an apostle and father of the faith.

Where would we be if these ones had not chosen the scary path?  While developing this book, I did a poll online to see which cover designs had the most appeal.  The one I loved that grabbed me first was rejected by most.  Do you want to know why?  They said it was too mysterious and too scary.  They all chose the graphic that looked bright, peaceful, and hunky-dory.  While I understand that's where we want to end up, it is not often where we start.

Most likely, we will find ourselves staring up into the mist like Isabelle, with a faint light ahead that beckons us to a brighter future.  And while I know it looks scary, trust me I know, I promise this path will be prove to be trustworthy in the end.

# Chapter 7:
# Frustrated or Accomplished

Edward couldn't imagine any other way of life. The sunlight shone through the groves of pine trees, as he slowly skied down the mountain. It was a gorgeous day to be on the slopes; and he wasn't in any hurry this morning, staying on back trails and as far away from the crowds as possible. This was his place of respite, a true escape from the reality he was avoiding.

Once upon a time, he had been an ambitious, young executive. He had pictured himself a superhuman of sorts, leaping any challenges and obstacles in a single bound. Naturally, he looked down on all of the subpar humans around him, who were not nearly as driven. *Oh yes, weren't those the days? You're such a poser, Edward. No one would believe that about you now*, suggested the frigid voice. The dark thoughts descended on him, knowing they'd found a vulnerable moment. *You've tried and failed at so many things; yours is a life of frustration,* they hissed.

The memories came flooding back, one fast on the heels of another. His first job promised to be amazing, or so they said. Edward had jumped in with both feet, working hard and striving to impress. Then came the fateful day he'd mentioned a legal standard in passing, one he felt they were failing to meet. With one simple, naïve mistake, he'd blacklisted himself. The rest of his days at that company were a blur: meetings with partners, lectures in back rooms, and pitying looks from coworkers who knew his days were numbered. *Yes, that's right; you were a horror show of mistakes despite all your efforts, why should you ever try again?* the icy accusations continued.

Leaning hard left, then right, Edward picked up speed, wishing the voices away. Faster and faster he skied, but the slideshow of his frustrated life simply wouldn't end. His next job had been a welcome reprieve, a chance to start again. His boss seemed kind and for once wasn't out to get him. However, it didn't take long to realize that he wasn't going anywhere fast in this position. This was a job where you earned the next rung simply by sticking around and gaining seniority. Trying here was also going to be a waste of time, so he began counting his days until he was out of there as well.

A few more of his feeble attempts flew by, almost as fast as his skis: more jobs with many more frustrations that had left him defeated. *All your friends have begun to accomplish great things, and here you are, running away and hiding because you don't have what it takes*. That last, brutal statement dug deep and began to sting incessantly. Edward leaned in even further, the wind whipping fiercely at his face. He was almost hoping one brutal crash would end it forever. The next moment, his left ski caught an edge, and he went head first over the tips.

Edward now found himself buried deeply in a snow bank. Ice and snow had ended up in all the wrong places, and who knew where his skis and poles ended up. *Just great buddy, you're an awesome skier too!* the chilly voice mocked. *Actually, this is quite appropriate. You're not just a failure at work you know…* The shadowy mist began to push memories toward his mind from other aspects of his past. "No!" Edward screamed.

It was too much; he couldn't take any more of the torturous accusations.

As he struggled to get his footing in the bottomless powder, he noticed a small snowflake drifting upward. Apart from the direction, he probably wouldn't have noticed it otherwise. It began to turn as it ascended, and with that angle, he noticed it also had a hint of gold. "What in the world," Edward mumbled. He continued digging around in the snow, in search of his lost equipment. When the downward slope produced nothing, he pushed his arms and legs against gravity and up the steep bank.

He had just caught a glimpse of one of his skis a few feet away, then another golden snowflake appeared. This one was quite a bit larger and astonishing in both its detail and shimmer. It was rotating upward, twisting this way and that. As the sun's rays shone through the myriad of crystals, he noticed a shadow of a word being projected onto the side of the mountain, just a few feet above him. Edward could hardly make out the word, "progressing." He watched the snowflake continue to drift, and with it, the word began to fade.

He whispered the word aloud one time before it might disappear forever. To his shock, the golden snowflake, as if on command, dropped out of the air and onto the snow. It formed a glistening silhouette, with the word "progressing" engraved on it. On a hunch, Edward extended his leg to the make-shift platform to see if it would hold in the snowy bank. Not only did it hold, he also felt a bit of bounce in the golden snowflake, as if it was spring loaded. *Progressing, progressing, could I actually be progressing?* he mused. Throwing his body weight forward onto the spring, he caught some air and flew a feet up the slope. This motion invigorated him, and he felt a surge of energy throughout his body.

Edward was able to grab his first ski and continue the search for the rest of his equipment. In so doing, his mind wandered to these odd snowflakes and what their message could possibly mean. Quick as these thoughts came, more golden flakes began gliding gently by. He could see the words "advancing," "succeeding," "uplifted," "fulfilled," and "accomplished" all being projected onto the mountainside above him. Each flake staggered from the others as they floated, almost like a sparkling staircase inviting him upward. He wasn't sure he could ever truly be accomplished after everything that had happened, but this enticement was hard to refuse.

*Don't be absurd! A golden staircase, now that's rich. You must really be losing it. They're going to lock you up in a psych ward at this rate*, cried the biting thoughts. The words on the snow began to fade, and the snowflakes were getting more distant as they continued to climb. Edward was convinced he had nothing to lose, so he ignored the clamor in his mind and put all of his energy toward that next flake, bravely uttering "I'm advancing." The dazzling snowflake immediately dropped, forming another shining platform for his ascent.

The draw upward was becoming stronger now, as he let each word cross his lips, followed by a stretch forward and a bounce. Edward last arrived on the golden snowflake platform that read "accomplished." His remaining ski and poles were now in his grasp, and the word felt so sure beneath his feet, as if it was always where he was meant to be. On all sides, he began to see shimmering glimpses of future opportunities that had seemed practically impossible. Standing up here though, they were easily within reach.

His hazel eyes followed the mountain downward to where he had first crashed into the snow bank. The outline of his body looked so far away, where he had been stuck and motionless not so many moments before. Though his ascent had been quick, he felt like a new man. From this perspective, the crash site looked so pitiful. Why had he ever chosen to stay in a low place, one of frustration, like the one on display below? Shaking off those old memories, Edward bent down and traced the word "accomplished" with his finger. With each letter and each golden flourish, he breathed in and out the possibilities of this new place. Then stepping into his skis, he began to prepare for an exhilarating descent.

\*\*\*

Edward had grown accustomed, too accustomed, with the lie that he would forever be unfulfilled and frustrated. No one expected much of anything from him anymore, so he didn't either. And while this state was less than ideal, it did protect him from the pain of the lack of accomplishment. Yet he wasn't shielded from the vicious thoughts that attacked his mind most days.

Like all of our characters, the suggestion that came of another way was so subtle, he could have easily missed it. The internal and external chaos we experience on a daily basis are sent for that reason: to deliberately keep us busy, so we don't see the path of truth that will lead us out. But on this day, he did catch it, a glimpse of another reality encapsulated in a golden snowflake. Here was his chance, an opportunity to alter his thinking so drastically, it would set him free forever.

**Now Enjoy the Show**

We have just about made it to the end of our journey here with the story of Edward. Along with our seven short stories, we also spent time discovering some powerful concepts. Let's give them a quick overview.

- We started by exploring the realities of the power of our yes and discussed the idea that what we believe will be end up being our experience.

- We also delved into the thought that the smallest of our internal choices are pivotal and acknowledged that free will is the most powerful thing we have.

- Next, we broke down what it looks like to take a courageous first step which will begin to shift the momentum in our favor.

- Then after that scary decision is made, it becomes hard to stop the runaway train of truth, because it does prove to be so trustworthy.

- After that final point, it simply becomes a matter of enjoying the show. By this I mean: sitting back and watching the fruits of your labor become reality, as the truths you have built your life upon begin to manifest.

So, do we feel like we've reached the point where we can truly enjoy the show?  Like actually, thoroughly enjoy?  I'm getting there, but haven't arrived yet fully.  We will know that confident enjoyment more and more, as we continue to cement God's truth in our hearts and reject the notions of lies that would enslave us.

I absolutely love the following quote from Steve Backlund. "The greatest strongholds blocking the purposes of God are not regional principalities, but rather the belief systems of people."  I certainly don't want to be part of the problem limiting what God wants to do on the earth in this generation, so I'm determined to keep my belief systems cleaned up and in alignment with Him.  I pray that you'll choose to join me on this golden path of truth.

# Epilogue:
# To the Reader

I am sure you noticed that none of our seven characters chose the dark path of lies. As I mentioned in the beginning, my desire to keep them in the light outweighed the desire to tell both sides of the story.

So while this didn't end up as a "choose your own adventure" tale, I hope that you can infer what would have transpired had our protagonists continued to listen to the frantic, icy voices. In your own life, you truly do have the power to choose your path.

I pray that this book enables you to make more right choices to agree with truth and stay in the light. Remember: This is what will unlock all possibilities for you and your family's future!

* * *

I hope you caught glimpses of your own journey as you read the stories here. Truth be told, there are bits and pieces of my life scattered throughout as well. These seven chapters represent some of the biggest lies people believe, the ones that can devastate a life and even take people out.

These were distilled down from a much larger listing of responses I received on a social media post from a few years ago. In Appendix I, you'll find the rest of the list, along with Scriptural rebuttals to combat every lie. I pray that this resource will allow you to break the often-subconscious hold of these thoughts and forge your way on to the path of truth instead! It would behoove us all to remember:

*For as he thinks in his heart, so is he.*

*–Proverbs 23:7*

# Appendix I:
# Dismantling Common
# Lies We Believe

1.  Lie: "I won't have what I need to survive"

    *Truth: I will have everything I need in this life to survive and thrive. I will not do without in any area of my existence. I break the agreement I have made with the lie of scarcity. Furthermore, I will even end up with excess that I can then pass along to others.*

    *Basis: "And my God will liberally supply (fill until full) your every need according to His riches in glory in Christ Jesus."*

    *—Philippians 4:19*

2.   Lie: "I will wither and die young"

*Truth: My life will reach the completion of my days. It will not be cut short by one moment. My body was created strong, and it does not wither. The life I will live will be one of flourishing, filled with all the energy and vigor I need to fulfill my purposes on the earth.*

*Basis: "He will call upon Me, and I will answer him; I will be with him in trouble; I will rescue him and honor him. With a long life I will satisfy him and I will let him see My salvation."*

*–Psalm 91:15-16*

3.   Lie: "My family will never make it, and I'll end up alone"

*Truth: God gifted me with this particular family, and it will operate as He originally intended. No issue will be too much for us to overcome. We are equipped and well able to stick together through thick and thin. We will walk in love and in unity, fighting for each other and supporting one another every day of our lives.*

*Basis: "A father of the fatherless and a judge and protector of the widows, is God in His holy habitation. God makes a home for the lonely; He leads the prisoners into prosperity, only the stubborn and rebellious dwell in a parched land."*

*–Psalm 68:5-6*

4.  Lie: "I'm not good enough, not worthy of love or belonging"

    *Truth: I am perfect exactly the way I am. I have been created on purpose, for a purpose. That purpose includes being loved by God, completely and thoroughly. I am worthy, because He says I am. I was good enough that He willingly gave up his lone Son, Jesus, for me. And He would do it again, even if only for me.*

    *Basis: "Because you are precious in My sight, you are honored and I love you, I will give other men in return for you and other peoples in exchange for your life."*

    *–Isaiah 43:4*

5.  Lie: "I have no value beyond what I do or provide to society"

    *Truth: I have intrinsic value, because I am made in the very image of Almighty God. Nothing I have done or will do can ever change that fact. God will never love me any more or any less than He does in this moment. My work becomes an extension of His goodness to me, and not a burden to bear to prove myself.*

    *Basis: "Yet You have made him a little lower than God, And You have crowned him with glory and honor. You made him to have the dominion over the works of Your hands; You have put all things under his feet."*

*—Psalm 8:5-6*

6.  <u>Lie: "My potential is limited because of my past"</u>

    *Truth: My past has been bought and paid for by the blood of Jesus Christ. I'm covered so well in fact, that this history has no bearing on my future. Going further, it's not even visible anymore. My potential is unlimited, as I walk forward hand-in-hand with God in freedom, humility, and mercy.*

    *Basis: "For as the heavens are high above the earth, so great is His loving kindness toward those who fear and worship Him (with awe-filled respect and deepest reverence). As far as the east is from the west, so far has He removed our transgressions from us."*

    *—Psalm 103:11-12*

7.  <u>Lie: "My best efforts always fail, so why try anymore"</u>

    *Truth: I resolve today that 'trying' will no longer be my posture. I don't just try; instead, I know that my efforts will succeed when I walk with God. Failure and frustration are in my past, and that is where they will stay. My future is bright with potential of all the things God and I will accomplish together.*

*Basis: "For we are His workmanship (His own master work a work of art), created in Christ Jesus (reborn from above, ready to be used) for good works, which God prepared (for us) beforehand, so that we would walk in them (living the good life which He prearranged and made ready for us)."*

*–Ephesians 2:10*

8.  Lie: "I am responsible & able to change others, making everyone/everything ok"

    *Truth: I am only responsible for me. Stepping outside of that boundary will only cause harm to myself and others. I will encourage, support, and pray for those to whom God assigns me, but I will not carry their load. Jesus is the only one whose shoulders are broad enough to carry us all, so I give them to Him now.*

    *Basis: "Take my yoke upon you and learn from Me (following Me as My disciple), for I am gentle and humble in heart, and you will find rest (renewal, blessed quiet) for your souls. For My yoke is easy (to bear) and My burden is light."*

    *–Matthew 11:29-30*

9. <u>Lie: "I believe I can find happiness through stuff or other people"</u>

   *Truth: I will only find true happiness and joy when I find God in the midst of the details of my life. My heart is hungry for something more, and He alone is that more. I will fill myself up with Him, instead of shallow substitutes, knowing that only then will I have anything to pass on to others.*

   *Basis: "But first and most importantly seek (aim at, strive after) His kingdom and His righteousness (his way of doing and being right – the attitude and character of God), and all these things will be given to you also."*

   *–Matthew 6:33*

10. <u>Lie: "Just one person can't make a difference"</u>

    *Truth: I know that one person can make an eternal difference, because Jesus did. He came to earth and lived as an ordinary man in order to redeem us from destruction. I will follow His example, choosing to obey God and submit my will, knowing that when I do, there will be great impact for the Kingdom.*

    *Basis: "The steps of a (good and righteous) man are directed and established by the Lord, and He delights in his way (and blesses his path). When he falls, he will not be hurled down, because the Lord is the One who holds his hand and sustains him."*

*–Psalm 37:23-24*

11. Lie: "I have to do it all by myself, & God won't help because I got myself into it"

*Truth: I am not an orphan, left alone to fend for myself. God is bigger than my mistakes. In fact, He sees the end from the beginning, so He has already carved out a way for me to get back on track. God will always help me and come to my aid, because He is a good and loving Father.*

*Basis: "If you then, evil (sinful by nature) as you are, know how to give good and advantageous gifts to your children, how much more will your Father who is in heaven (perfect as He is) give what is good and advantageous to those who keep on asking Him."*

*–Matthew 7:11*

12. Lie: "God CAN do anything, but He won't do it for me"

*Truth: I am God's child, His creation, and His delight. The immensity of His nature is available to me. This is because Jesus paid the price for me to be accepted in the beloved forever. I am not worth more or less than other people. We all are equals at the foot of the cross.*

*Basis: "And He raised us up together with Him (when we believed), and seated us with Him in the heavenly places, (because we are) in Christ Jesus. So that in the ages to come He might (clearly) show the immeasurable and unsurpassed riches of His grace in kindness toward us in Christ Jesus."*

*–Ephesians 2:6-7*

13. <u>Lie: "I cannot handle what lies ahead"</u>

*Truth: I will not dread what I cannot see. The days ahead will be better than the ones that came before. Instead of walking in dread, I will confidently ask God to strengthen me as I face each new season. He is good and always with me. If He sits in the heavens and laughs, then so can I.*

*Basis: "He who sits (enthroned) in the heavens laughs (at their rebellion); The (Sovereign) Lord scoffs at them (and in supreme contempt He mocks them)."*

*–Psalm 2:4*

14. <u>Lie: "My faith isn't enough for a miracle"</u>

*Truth: I will not hang on to my prayers too tightly in self-effort. I trust that God, who is*

*Lord of the harvest, will bring them to pass. I will take my mustard seed of faith and believe. Then, I will rely on the faith and the power of Jesus alone to bring about the victory in my life. I lean into His character as the Almighty.*

*Basis: "For God alone my soul waits in silence and quietly submits to Him, for my hope is from Him. He only is my rock and my salvation; my fortress and my defense, I will not be shaken or discouraged. On God my salvation and my glory rest; He is my rock of (unyielding) strength, my refuge is in God."*

*–Psalm 62:5-7*

15. Lie: "I don't think there will be consequences for my actions"

    *Truth: The choices I make will have tangible effects in the here and now, for good or for bad. This is an eternal principle, and I am not exempt from it. God will graciously help me out of my mess when I turn to Him, but I will have more bumps in the road if I choose to go my own way.*

    *Basis: "Enter through the narrow gate. For wide is the gate and broad and easy to travel is the path that leads the way to destruction and eternal loss, and there are many who enter through it".*

*–Matthew 7:13*

16. <u>Lie: "I believe that God is like my abusive parent"</u>

    *Truth: My life may have had some poor examples, including my parents.  However, I will not take that as evidence of God's character.  He is perfect and complete, lacking in nothing.  My understanding of His goodness and kindness will continue to grow as I separate my human conceptions from his divine nature.*

    *Basis: "Lord, You have been our dwelling place (our refuge, our sanctuary, our stability) in all generations.  Before the mountains were born or before You had given birth to the earth and the world, even from everlasting to everlasting, You are (the eternal) God."*

    *–Psalm 90:1-2*

17. <u>Lie: "I have to have it all together and fake it until I make it"</u>

    *Truth: There is no requirement for me to have it all together.  God accepts my imperfections, and the people who truly love me will too.  I reject the idea that being fake will move me forward in life.  Transparency and vulnerability are actually more attractive and provide more favor.*

*Basis: "But above all, my fellow believers, do not swear, either by heaven or by earth or with any other oath; but let your yes be (a truthful) yes, and your no be (a truthful) no, so that you may not fall under judgment."*

*—James 5:12*

18. Lie: "I'm JUST a sinner saved by grace"

*Truth: I will not claim an identity that names me with the enemy's camp. I am part of God's original intent, His perfect creation. Though corrupted by a heritage of sin, through Jesus, I have been restored to my rightful place. Now I occupy the place created for me since before the foundations of the world.*

*Basis: "But God, being (so very) rich in mercy, because of His great and wonderful love with which He loved us, even when we were (spiritually) dead and separated from Him because of our sins, He made us (spiritually) alive together with Christ."*

*—Ephesians 2:4-5*

19. Lie: "Worry and negative thoughts will control my life"

*Truth: I can and will overcome worry. It is not my portion, and I refuse to accept it. With my whole heart, I will set my focus on God's truth.*

*From that standard, worry cannot exist and loses its place. My life will be controlled instead by the atmosphere of the Kingdom, which is righteousness, peace, and joy.*

*Basis: "And who of you by worrying can add one hour to (the length of) his life? So do not worry about tomorrow; for tomorrow will worry about itself. Each day has enough trouble of its own."*

*—Matthew 6:27,34*

20. <u>Lie: "I can handle everything without anyone's help, especially God"</u>

*Truth: I am limited in my human abilities in this earthbound realm. The restraints of time and space, however, are no match for the infiniteness of God. It's not a sign of weakness to rely on Him. Rather, it's a marker of wisdom. I will gladly enlist the help of my omnipotent, omnipresent, omniscient God who loves me.*

*Basis: "For He knows our (mortal) frame; He remembers that we are (merely) dust. But the loving kindness of the Lord is from everlasting to everlasting on those who (reverently) fear Him, and His righteousness to children's children."*

*—Psalm 103:14,17*

21. Lie: "God doesn't answer my prayers the way I like anyway, so why pray"

    *Truth: I will keep praying even if I don't get what I want. Just like an adult knows more than a child, I trust that my good God who exceeds me on every possible metric, is answering my prayers to a "T." I believe that He knows the desires of my heart, and with patience, my inheritance will arrive in completion and on-time.*

    *Basis: "Trust in and rely confidently on the Lord with all your heart and do not rely on your own insight or understanding. In all your ways know and acknowledge and recognize Him, and He will make your paths straight and smooth (removing obstacles that block your way)."*

    *–Proverbs 3:5-6*

22. Lie: "I should just do what makes me feel happy"

    *Truth: I can delay instant gratification when I need to. Although it may stretch me, I will put my big-kid pants on and look to the end result. I can have the long-view of time, as God does. I will choose not to focus on my short-term whims, but be clever and strategic in prioritizing my life.*

*Basis: "He has made everything beautiful and appropriate in its time. He has also planted eternity (a sense of divine purpose) in the human heart (a mysterious longing which nothing under the sun can satisfy, except God)."*

*—Ecclesiastes 3:11*

## 23. Lie: "I can and should have it all"

*Truth: I won't set unreasonable expectations on this life, which will cause me to run at a frenzied, chaotic pace. I acknowledge my circumstances honestly and make wise choices as to how to order my days, regardless of those around me. I will look forward to the day in eternity when we truly will have it all!*

*Basis: "Nevertheless, do not let this one fact escape your notice, beloved, that with the Lord one day is like a thousand years, and a thousand years is like one day. The Lord does not delay and is not slow about His promise, as some count slowness, but is extraordinarily patient toward you."*

*—2 Peter 3:8-9*

## 24. Lie: "All GOOD people will go to heaven"

*Truth: I know that the only path to my goodness is through Jesus. His death and resurrection are what transform me from a sin-nature to a heavenly-nature. If I don't believe in Him, any perceived goodness I have is shallow and self-serving at best. I understand that the only way to heaven is by calling on His name!*

*Basis: "Jesus said to him, "I am the (only) Way (to God) and the (real) Truth and the (real) Life; no one comes to the Father but through me."*

*—John 14:6*

# Appendix II:
# Daily Living on the Path of Truth

## *Practice 1*

JOT DOWN THE
*Various parts*
OF YOUR LIFE INTO TWO LISTS:
1) THOSE ALIVE WITH LIGHT AND LIFE OR
2) THOSE SHROUDED IN HOPELESS DARKNESS

*We can have very different results in the various arenas of our lives. You may have a very 'successful' family but have never been able to break through to favor in your workplace. We all have our own stories and distinct lies that hold us back.*

*Perhaps a good start to finding the path of truth would be to jot down which areas of our lives are alive with life & light and which areas are shrouded in hopeless darkness. Once we've spotted the lies, we can whittle them down with truth.*

## *Practice 2*

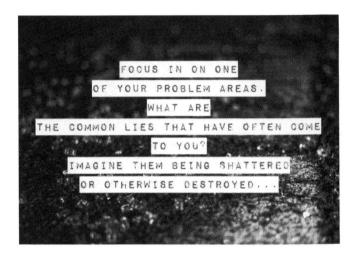

*Focus in on one trouble area filled with lies. Take a moment to jog your memory. What are the common lies you hear repeated about this part of your life? If we pay attention, there's definitely a theme, if not exact phrases, that are used over and over.*

*Now that you've accessed those lies, picture them being broken, shattered, or otherwise destroyed. Your imagination is a powerful tool in this regard. Remember, the enemy's cover has been blown. Let that be your focus when the lies try to return.*

## *Practice 3*

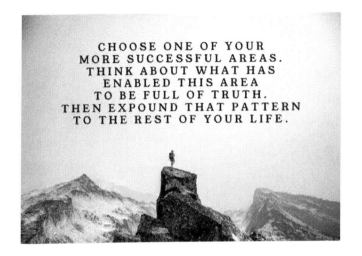

*Choose one of your more successful areas that is dominated by truth. What about this part of your existence makes it easy to believe truth? Have you always been successful in this venue? Does your family history lean toward strength in this area?*

*Once you've come to some conclusion about the anointing of ease in this particular area, journal what it would look like to transfer this ability into the other problem areas of your life as well.*

## *Practice 4*

SELECT A SCRIPTURE TO GET YOUR MIND OFF
THE LIES AND ON THE BIGGER PICTURE.
FIND A CREATIVE WAY TO
REMEMBER THIS VERSE.

*Select a Scripture that best helps you get your mind off of the lies amidst the fray. This would be a passage that elevates your perspective and helps you see the bigger picture into eternity, rather than the daily struggle for truth.*

*Design a creative way to commit this verse to memory and keep it close at hand. Write a little jingle, make a meme on your phone, color it onto a note card. The eternal truth of the Word of God puts the temporal urgency of lies in their rightful place.*

## *Practice 5*

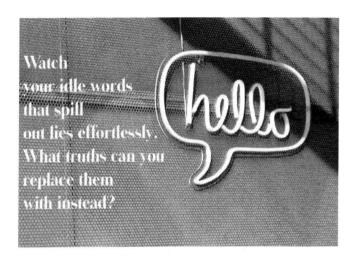

*As you go through your day, pay attention to the idle words that come out of your mouth. Just like a vehicle, these are moments when you're running but not actually moving. Casual things can slip out of our mouths that are good, but others can be downright frightening.*

*Once you've heard a few of the negatives (and I'm sure we all will), stop and assess why they're so readily accessible for you. Did you hear your parents say them? Are they from some media you can remove from your life? Take a mental note to replace those slippery phrases with a truth to be uttered instead.*

*Practice 6*

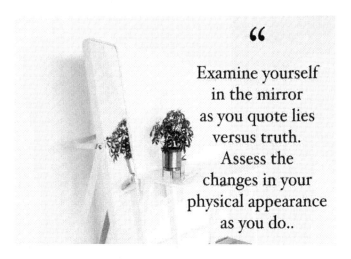

> Examine yourself in the mirror as you quote lies versus truth. Assess the changes in your physical appearance as you do..

*Examine yourself in the mirror. Choose several of the big lies you've identified throughout the reading of this book. Repeat them out loud as you observe your face. Note your body language, mood, and posture as you confess these words.*

*Now grab some of the truths you've started to focus on and state these to yourself in the mirror. What is the difference in your physical appearance, voice tone, and emotional state when you repeat these phrases?*

## *Practice 7*

THINK ABOUT
YOUR FAVORITE
CREATIVE
EXPRESSIONS.
WHAT TRUTH HAVE THESE
BEEN COMMUNICATING
TO YOUR SOUL?

*Spend some time thinking about your favorite art, songs, movies, etc. Is there a consistent theme or message woven throughout these creative works?*

*Record your thoughts as to the eternal truths that may be contained in these. What part of them is resonating with your soul and drawing you in? It's probably a truth you need to hear, focus on, and live out.*

# Redeem Your Free Gift

*We would like to give you these two appendixes in electronic format, so you can keep them handy and forward them on to friends and family*

*Head over to www.AndreaJoy.org/Truth and subscribe today to receive these files in pdf format*

# Reviews

*Reader feedback is incredibly helpful for authors. Would you please consider taking the time to write a review on www.amazon.com?*

**Grateful for You!**

# About the Author

Andrea Joy Moede is a recovering over achiever who has traveled a long road of transformation. While she grew up in an amazing, believing family, she was ultimately left still searching for God. This was because she hadn't yet made the shift from dutiful religion to passionate relationship. As a young person, she set out to conquer the world with full scholarships to Texas A&M's business school and SMU's law school. When law school didn't quite fit the bill, she embarked on a career in accounting and finance at KPMG, Valero Energy, and USAA. She finally ended up spending time in an accounting PhD program at

the University of Texas at San Antonio.

During this period, she was running from God and trying to determine her own destiny, before finally realizing that life on His path was so much better than anywhere else. She came to this understanding during the unexpectedly quiet years of being a young stay at home mom.

Now she is only determined to be a receiver of God's love and provision and to follow wherever He leads. She is excited about helping people come into the fullness of both their identity and calling and believes that this is best accomplished by beholding God in all of His fullness first.

When not writing, you can catch her busy with some of her favorite things - highly doctored coffee, endorphin inducing workouts, schmaltzy movies, long naps on rainy days, really good Italian food, coaching her kids sports teams, and sitting down with just about any book.

She lives in the San Antonio area with her husband – Austen, their two busy boys, and their equally busy baby girl. They enjoy being a part of what God is doing at Bethel Austin and throughout the hill country. When not enduring the climate of South Texas, they all prefer to escape to the mountains.

Connect with the author at www.AndreaJoy.org.

Made in the USA
Columbia, SC
10 March 2020